To Cam

I hope y...

Nick Le Mesurier

A Song for the Ferryman

and other tales from ancient times

Re-told by
Nick Le Mesurier

For Kate

Copyright @ 2018 Nick Le Mesurier
All rights reserved.

Contents

Preface 1
Melusine 8
The Raven and the Crow 43
Isabella and the Business of Business 53
A Dream in Paradise 65
A Song for the Ferryman 92
The Raven's Command 101

Preface

I've long had a fascination for tales. And what better tales are there than some of the ancient ones? The older the better, one might say. The Greeks and Romans knew how to tell a good tale, and so did the medieval world which often drew upon such ancient sources.

In seeking to find threads in these ancient tapestries that tie in with some of our own concerns, particularly the identity and status of women, I have found a rich source of material that with only the slightest of twists meets the needs of today. Each is intended to be read aloud or even performed, though I hope they will give as much pleasure on the page.

Melusine is a case in point. Her origins lie far back in the European memory. She is a female both human and serpent, a not uncommon conflation in ancient times, reflecting perhaps an ambiguous but nevertheless powerful sexuality - and no doubt men's own anxiety in the face of it. Her demands for time and space of her own apart from men's gaze certainly chimes with women's demands to be seen, not just as more than sex-objects defined and created by men, but as individuals defined on their own terms. My version of the story needed only to depart a little from the many ancient versions to find its relevance.

Ovid was one of the greatest poets of love, and he had a sharp eye for the shifts in power that occur in relationships. *The Raven and the Crow* is a parable taken from *Metamorphoses*, again only slightly altered to make a point that is as relevant today as it was more than two thousand years ago.

Boccaccio is another source without which Western literature would be infinitely poorer. His *Decameron*, consisting of a hundred tales told by a group of Florentine noble men and women biding their time by telling stories to each other till the plague has left the city, is a rich source of material for anyone wanting to know the workings of the human heart. In *Isabella and the Business of Business* I have taken the well-known story of *Lisabetta and the Pot of Basil* and again given it a modern twist. Far from being the pale sister who robs her dead lover of his heart and then hides it beneath a pot of basil before subsiding into terminal grief, my Isabella is a sharp-minded individual who finds that by working with the status quo she can turn it to her own advantage and thus create an identity and a power that is hers alone.

Another fate befalls Andreola in my second tale from Boccaccio's stable, which I call *A Dream in Paradise*. Her love for the handsome Gabriotto arguably brings about his death and her downfall, though it is really guilt and the moral codes of the day that bedevil their affair. Nevertheless she, too, finds a kind of identity after tragedy.

A Song for the Ferryman returns to the classical world and to Ovid in particular to steal another ancient tale, that of *Orpheus and Eurydice*, this time given a comic twist. It proves the point, I hope, that sometimes an old tale can be given new life by telling it in the voice of one of the original minor characters who might otherwise be overlooked. So Orpheus slips out of the hands of Ovid and Purcell into the heady world of rock and roll, and Charon gets to meet one of his heroes.

Finally *The Raven's Command* is a confection of my own, written as a script which I hope you will find reads as well on the page as it might on the stage. We could not have a book of ancient stories without having that arch-villain and master of disguises, the Devil, play a part. Not that he needs to do much to let the dark side of human nature take flight.

Melusine

Once, long ago, when the worlds of the spirits and of men and women were not so far apart, there lived a king, called Elinas. Now, Elinas had a wife who bore him a son; but his wife had died, and he grieved mightily for her. To console himself he often went hunting, and on one of these hunts he came across a beautiful young woman sitting beside a pool. Her name was Pressyne, and she had beautiful long golden hair.

'Why do you sit here, gazing into these waters,' said the king.

'What is it you see there?'

The woman thought for a moment. 'I see the future,' she said, for she recognised the king as a man still handsome and in the prime of life.

'And what do you see of the future,' said the king, 'for I have lately lost the woman I love and I can see nothing?'

'I see a bright new morning,' she said, 'and great prosperity in the kingdom. All will be well as long as peace shall reign.'

The king was so enchanted by her answer and by her lovely long tresses that he asked her if she would marry him. The young woman hesitated, and then said: 'I will be pleased to marry you and to share your bed, but I must insist upon one condition.'

'What is that?' said the king, who, in the way of fairy tales, had fallen instantly in love with her and was ready to grant her anything she wished.

'I must insist that I have my own chambers where I shall never be observed by you or by any man. This request must be solemnly observed without question. In all other respects I will be your wife and share your throne and your bed, and we shall see great prosperity together.'

The king felt he was in no position to argue, and saw no problem in agreeing to her wishes, especially as she offered great prosperity. So, he agreed, and they were married within a month. Soon she gave birth, and not to one child but three! They named them Melusine, Melior, and Palatyne.

Now, the king had a son from his first marriage, who like many such children was not pleased that his father had married again, for he did not want to share power or influence over him. So, he questioned his step-mother at every turn, and he tried to spread false rumours, particularly about her command that she be not observed when in her own quarters.

'It is not natural,' he said, 'for a woman to lay down such conditions upon her husband, and particularly a king, who should have the right to gaze upon whoever he chose. There must be some trick going on. Perhaps she is not alone?'

Now, Elinas loved his new wife and saw no great need or urgency to question her wish. After all, she had borne him three daughters and seemed to love him in every way a wife should. Moreover, the kingdom was indeed flourishing, as she had promised. And so he refused to listen to his son's gossip and intrigue.

But the son was not so easily dissuaded, and the more his father insisted on his wife's innocence the more the young man was convinced of her guilt.

Finally, the king said, 'Will it end your doubts if I take one look and report to you what I see? Will that end your ceaseless tittle tattle?'

The son agreed, and so that night Elinas crouched down at

the keyhole to the door of his wife's chamber while she bathed with her three daughters, and saw to his surprise and horror that while she was naked and as lovely as ever from the waist up, below she had not legs but a huge serpent's tale that swished and thrashed about in the water.

It was such a shock to him that in rising he knocked over a vase that was standing nearby. The sound immediately alerted Pressyne, and by an instinct she knew that it was her beloved husband that had betrayed her. She said nothing at the time, but one night while he was sleeping she gathered up her children and stole out of the palace and escaped to another land, leaving a note saying that she had asked only one promise of him and he had broken it, and thus he would see her no more. She left him a lock of her lovely golden hair to remember her by.

And so it came to be, for no matter where he looked, no matter how far his spies travelled, he learned nothing of their whereabouts. And though this might seem strange to us, to him it seemed inevitable, for had it not turned out he had married a water spirit, albeit inadvertently, and such beings could slip away wherever they wished, as easily as water though a grate. Pressyne, however, had not vanished but had escaped to an island far away where she and her daughters managed to build a new life for themselves; and if she thought of her husband it was with some sorrow, but also the conviction that she had been right to do what she had done, for a solemn promise is a solemn promise and it shouldn't be broken without consequence.

Now, things were not always easy for Pressyne and her girls in their new home, and sooner or

later they fell upon hard times.
One day Melusine, who was the
eldest of the three girls, asked
her mother why they should
have to suffer like this without a
father to support them. At first
Pressyne tried to pass off her
daughter's demands, but as she
was persistent she sat them
down and told them the story.

'You see,' she said, 'your
father made a promise and he
broke it. And my secret, which
you know, was revealed. I could
not risk what might happen to
you if the people got to hear of
my true identity, for they are very
superstitious and I knew that no-

one would be safe, not you, nor I, nor even your father would be spared. And so, we escaped, and thus we have lived, without riches it is true, but in peace.'

'That's outrageous!' exclaimed Melusine with all the righteousness of youth. 'How could you let our father get away with it? He has done nothing to support us, and look at us now: we are poor, we are hungry, we are cold, and we could have lived like the princesses we are. This is all your fault!'

'I know,' said her mother. 'But its better this way, believe me.'

'Well, I don't think so!' said

Melusine.

Melusine said nothing more about it to her mother, for she knew that once her mind was made up nothing would change it. But she resolved with her sisters to go to visit their father and confront him with the truth and to demand he give them what was rightly theirs.

And so, one night they stole away and travelled many days and nights to their father's palace where one morning they presented themselves at the palace gates.

'Tell our father that his daughters are here to see him,'

she said. When the guards told the king of the strange women who had showed up at his gate he rushed down to see them, full of hope that they might indeed be his daughters. And though he had not seen them since they were babies, he recognised them at once and he gathered them up in his arms and wept with joy to have them home again. And they too were overcome with happiness to see their father. Together they went into the great palace, and the king begged to know where Pressyne was. At first the girls would not tell him, but soon they relented and told him where they had been living.

'So close!' he said. 'And I never knew. But that is just like my Pressyne. We will go to her straight away and bring her back. For I am truly sorry for my sin and wish to make amends.'

The girls readily agreed, but Melusine insisted that they go ahead of him to prepare their mother, for she suspected she might not take well to the surprise of him turning up unannounced. The king agreed, and sent the girls off with an escort to see them safely home.

When they got back their mother was overjoyed to see

them, for they had simply left a note explaining they were off on an expedition. Then the girls explained:

'We went see our father,' they said. 'He is well and he misses us terribly, and he sends his love and we have told him where we live so that he can come and rescue us and we can all be happy together again.'

On hearing this Pressyne became very angry. 'What have you done!' she cried. 'I told you never to contact him again. I made my decision when he broke his promise, and I had hoped you would respect that.

But now I see you are not to be trusted either.' And with that she threatened to curse her daughters.

Now it is a terrible thing for a mother to curse her daughters. So Melusine reached forward and said, 'Mother, it was not my sisters but I that planned this. I merely took them along for company. If anyone is to be cursed it must be me alone.'

'Very well,' said Pressyne, 'since you ask it, you shall be the one to take the blame. But this is no ordinary curse. For each Saturday night from now on, you will know your true self. You shall be as I am, and if you are wise you will do all you can to keep yourself from the prying eyes of men, who seek in their looks to take from you that which is yours.' And with that Melusine gave a painful cry, and she looked down and saw she had developed a beautiful serpent's tale instead of legs.

'And now, said Pressyne, 'we must go. We must not be found together, for though the king might welcome us, others will not, and we will lose our freedom, and maybe even our very lives.' And with that she twirled her hands above her head and caused a great wind to blow them far away.

Melusine awoke to find herself alone in a forest in a strange land with all her limbs restored to her as before. She looked around but there was nothing there she could recognise. So, she started to walk and soon she found a stream that led to a little pool, and there she sat down and gazed into the waters and wondered what she should do.

It wasn't long before she was disturbed by a loud rustling noise and the sounds of hunting. Suddenly she saw an old man stagger out of the bushes with an arrow in his chest, who fell down dead at her feet. No sooner had the breath left his body than another man burst out of the bushes with a bow in his hand. This man was young and handsome, but when he saw the old man's body lying dead upon the ground he fell back, trembling.

'What have I done, what have I done?' cried the young man.

'I'd say you've shot him,' said Melusine, curious at what had happened.

'Indeed, I have,' said the young man. 'And when the rest

of the party find him they will know it was me and they will kill me.'

'Why?' said Melusine.

'Because he's my uncle,' said the young man.

'Did you mean to kill him?' said Melusine.

'No,' said the young man. 'Though to be honest I'm not sorry. He never liked me.'

Melusine saw that this young man, who looked every inch a prince, could help turn her fortunes. So, she quickly worked out a plan.

'Come with me,' she said. 'Let us move swiftly to another part of the forest. There we will lie and I will say you were with me all the time and could not possibly have fired the shot that killed your uncle. Come!'

The prince could not think of a better plan, and though he couldn't see quite why his luck should have so suddenly turned, he took the opportunity, as any lusty young fellow would, and ran with her swiftly through the bushes to a place where they lay down together.

'Make love to me,' said Melusine, 'and then they will know you could not have shot your uncle.'

So, he did. And he found her to be a marvellous lover, skilled and passionate and to his amazement seemingly in love with him. When the king and his courtiers found him they humbly apologised for disturbing them and told him that his uncle was dead, killed by someone, who even now was paying the price for his deed.

The prince, who was called Raymond, could hardly believe his luck. Not only had he rid himself of his nasty uncle but he had discovered a beautiful woman who appeared to wish him only good. And when she boldly declared to the king and his courtiers that the prince had proposed to her he could hardly argue or deny what would soon become fact.

    And so they were wed. It was a grand ceremony, and everyone complemented Raymond on his beautiful wife. But as soon as they were alone together she said to Raymond, 'I am now your wife, and I will serve you with all my heart and with all my mind and with all the talents at my command, and together we will make this kingdom rich. But I will do this on one condition only.'

'What's that?' said the prince.

'For six days of the week I will be yours entirely, but each Saturday night I demand I must be on my own. You will neither see me nor hear me nor know anything of what I do. And I promise I will be true to you, always, and ask only that you trust me and faithfully observe my wish, as I will faithfully observe my vows to you. I ask you to swear this to me on your honour.'

Raymond looked puzzled at this request and asked her, 'Why do you want this?'

'You don't need to know,'

Melusine replied. 'Only remember that I helped you once, and I can help you again.'

The prince could see that it would be wise to accept her terms, no matter how bizarre they might seem. So, he swore.

And Melusine was true to her word. When the king died Raymond took over the throne, and with her wits she helped him build a new kingdom, greater than the one he had inherited. Their lands grew, and their armies grew, and their riches grew; and so did their family, for they had many children, who, as they came of age were married into some of the greatest families in Europe, so that peace reigned throughout the continent.

But – and there is always a but – after a while some people became suspicious of Melusine's strange behaviour on a Saturday night. They remarked that she was never to be seen then, and did not appear even when her husband was entertaining royalty on some state occasion. Some, who were jealous of her power, even said she was a witch and that she withdrew each Saturday night to practice spells, which were the reason for the kingdom's prosperity.

Then, for reasons best known to herself, Melusine suddenly declared that she would no longer attend Mass on a Sunday. This was shocking to many people and confirmed that she was, after all, a witch and up to no good.

Now, as you know, gossip never diminishes, not when it has a good mystery to feed upon, and so little bit by little bit the pressure grew upon the king to find out what Melusine was up to. The fact that Melusine's wisdom and good counsel had provided so many benefits to the kingdom seemed increasingly irrelevant to this rising tide of gossip, and eventually the king was persuaded that he must know the truth.

And so he did as Pressyne's husband had done, and broke his vow. He looked upon his wife through the keyhole to her private chambers one Saturday night. And just as Elinas had done, so he saw his lovely wife, as beautiful as ever from the waist up, but as a serpent down below.

Now, history does not always turn in neat circles, and this time Melusine was unaware of the betrayal, until the actions of their son led to calamity. It happened like this.

This son, by the name of Geoffrey, had a peculiar deformity of temperament, which drove him to get into many fights. Even as a small child he could terrorise his masters, and other children quickly learned not to play with him. As he grew he became more isolated and more bad tempered, and he gained a reputation as a dangerous man to be around; a good ally in battle, perhaps, but a deadly foe when crossed. Nevertheless, his fearsome reputation served the kingdom well, for along with peace and good government, his father could call upon his services when he needed to defend or attack some cause. Thus, Geoffrey remained a canker in the land, feared by most people and unloved by all, except his mother.

In one of Geoffrey's periodic fits of ill-temper he set fire to the grand cathedral in the middle of the capital city. No-one knew why he did it, and everyone was quick to blame him and to say, 'Enough is enough: he must be banished!' But Melusine defended him and forbade her husband from punishing the boy. And this for the first time caused a great rift between them, to which the people quickly took sides, either for Raymond or for his son Geoffrey. Each side accused Melusine of witchcraft and of having undue influence over the king.

Raymond could not ignore the demands of his people to rid himself of his dear wife; and she did not make matters easier by accusing each side of treason. So uncomfortable did Raymond's position become that one day he angrily confessed that he knew her true nature and what she did on those days that she insisted were her own, and that her wits were like those of a serpent.

Melusine instantly knew she had been betrayed, just as her mother had been, by a man she thought she could trust. She let out a terrible shriek as her form changed to that of a huge serpent and she flew out of the window, thrashing her long scaly tail behind her.

Soon news of her change went about, and with it the belief that if she were ever seen again, death would surely follow. And so indeed it came to pass.

Some people rallied in support of Geoffrey, some in support of Raymond, and it was not long before civil war erupted. Geoffrey gathered a great army and openly challenged his father; but in the ensuing fight Geoffrey was killed and his father's side was victorious. And there were those who said, long after, that while the battle raged it was as if a great serpent was seen in the midst of them, rushing between the two sides, striking out at each.

Raymond may have won the war, but he was a broken man. He had no appetite any more to be king, and a deal was quickly struck whereby the crown would pass to his eldest son who had married a neighbouring princess. Raymond went into voluntary exile and died quietly a few years later, having found some peace in a remote monastery. Their offspring went on to found some of the greatest royal families on the continent.

And for many, many years afterwards, till people lost faith in the world of the spirits, there were those who said that from time to time Melusine would revisit the kingdom searching for her children, and that her cries could be heard in the wind as it shrieked around the chimneys in a storm.

The Raven and the Crow

Once upon a time the great god Apollo, god of music, poetry, and a whole lot else besides, had a special pet, a raven, who because he was so nosey served as his spy. And in those days ravens were white, as white as snow.

Now, Apollo had taken a mortal, named Coronis as a lover. She was quite a looker and Apollo doted on her, but she was not quite so much in love with him, and so wasn't as faithful as she might have been. Heaven being quite a small place it wasn't long before the raven got to hear of this, and he immediately set off to report it to his master.

On his way he was interrupted by his cousin, a crow who like him had a hunger for intrigue, and who could see that something was clearly afoot. So she stopped him and demanded to know what was going on. And the raven, feeling he could trust one of his own kin, told her the dreadful secret.

'Don't do it!' cried the crow after she'd heard him out. 'You'll only regret it.'

The raven looked quite startled. 'Why?' he said.

'Once I was as white as you are now,' said the crow, ruffling her feathers, 'But now I'm as black as night.'

The raven had a beak for intrigue and sensed a juicy story. 'I wondered how that happened,' he said.

'I once saw a meeting in which my mistress Minerva hid a baby inside a basket and entrusted it to the care of three young women with strict instructions not to peek inside. Well, I could have told her what would happen.'

'I think I can guess.' said the raven, 'But do go on.'

'I followed the women. Two of them were sensible,' said the crow, 'but the third one opened the basket.'

'It's always the third one,' said the raven.

The crow nodded sagely. She paused for effect.

'And?' said the raven after a while.

'And what?' said the crow. 'I told my mistress the truth of what I'd seen. And that was my mistake.'

'Why,' said the raven.

'I thought she liked me,' said the crow, nibbling at one of her claws. 'I thought she'd be glad to know.'

'I'm surprised,' said the raven, warming to her subject. 'You told us once how you and she had this 'special thing'; how you were like sisters; how she never went anywhere without you; and how there were no secrets between you. I never did believe it myself.'

'All right, all right!' said the crow. 'So I misjudged her. It was an honest mistake.'

'Of course it was, dear' said the raven. 'Still, no smoke without fire, that's what I say. Is that why she turned you black and kicked you out?'

'All I'd done was tell her the truth,' said the crow sadly, 'which is what she employed me to do in the first place. But there are truths that gods want to hear and truths they don't.'

'What do you mean?' said the raven.

'I tell you, there's no virtue left in this world when an honest bird can be brought down for doing her job.'

The raven shook his head. 'I don't think I've heard such a load of stuff and nonsense in all my born days. And I don't believe your story about your dismissal. I think you're hiding something. In my book, if you've done nothing wrong you've got nothing to fear, and that's all there is to it. So I'm off to see my friend Apollo. Good day!' And with this he rudely brushed the poor crow aside and hurried off to complete his mission.

When the raven delivered his message to Apollo that great god was thunderstruck. You wouldn't think that one of the mightiest of the immortals could be brought down by a simple tale of infidelity, but he was - notwithstanding he'd had a few affairs himself. I do believe he had genuinely loved Coronis, and her betrayal cut him deeply to the heart. But Apollo was always Apollo, and he had a fearsome temper. So he took his bow and he shot an arrow straight through Coronis's heart.

As soon as he had done it he regretted it, but it was too late. As she lay dying she spoke words that shocked him to the core. 'I'm so sorry for my betrayal my love,' she said, 'And you are right to seek revenge on me. But I only wish you'd waited, for I am carrying your child, that now will never be born.'

At this Apollo wept and cried

aloud and immediately ordered the grandest of funeral ceremonies. It went on for a week. And just as he was about to place her body on the funeral pyre he took a knife and cut open her belly and drew forth his son, whom he entrusted to Chiron, the centaur, who had been his teacher and his guide. And I'm glad to say the lad turned out well. He became a doctor, Aesculapius, the god of medicine in fact, so the end wasn't all bad.

But things did not go so well for the raven. For though Apollo was struck down by grief he was still a god, and like all gods he was unwilling to take responsibility for his actions. So he cursed his poor pet and turned him to the deepest shade of black and banished him to the lonely hills, where you'll find him to this day.

Isabella and the Business of Business

Once, not so long ago, as I have heard, there lived in this town two brothers and their younger sister. They were born into a wealthy family, but their parents had died shortly after the brothers came of age.

Now, the brothers managed everything to do with the businesses and left their sister, who was called Isabella, to do more or less as she pleased. They gave her some education and openly planned for her to make a good marriage which would bring them greater wealth. Isabella gave every impression of being a typical young woman of her class. She loved nothing more than to buy fine clothes, play music, and visit friends and to take pleasure in all the gossip of the city. But she was also a shrewd observer and shared her brother's love of money and politics, and whenever she could she listened in on their discussions about business, and she learned a great deal from them. And as their business interests grew the brothers found they needed an agent to help them manage their affairs. They searched high and low and took great care in their selection. Eventually they settled upon a young man whose name was Lorenzo. He had learned his craft in some of the best houses in the region and was aware of his skills, and he was easily tempted by a generous offer.

As soon as the young couple saw each other a spark passed between them of the kind no amount of good sense and high morals can quell. Day by day as he settled into his new job she observed him, and soon she found an excuse to confront him. Whereupon their talk quickly turned to matters of the heart and they found the need to seek those moments that only couples who are deeply and passionately in love can know and create.

Their love making was full-blooded and joyful, and was more or less an open secret in the house. It might have gone well for the couple, but Lorenzo had no wealth of his own and Isabella's brothers had in mind for her a much more lucrative marriage. So it was not long before they called an urgent meeting to discuss what should be done.

'We must act circumspectly,' said one of them. 'It will not do us much good to be seen to have allowed this fellow to exceed his limits.'

'Better to deal with the matter quietly, and then marry her off as soon as possible,' said the other.

So they agreed to send Lorenzo on a business trip to a far off city and there arrange an accident that would rid them of the problem in one fell stroke. Matters went as planned, and when he failed to return they explained his absence by an excuse to do with business. Then they reported that he had died of an illness and had been hastily buried.

The news deeply affected Isabella, and she fell into mourning, weeping copiously for days on end over her loss, which of course she could not declare. Seeing the need to act swiftly, the brothers informed her that they had found a wealthy suitor who was keen to marry her and of whom they approved because of his many and useful business interests. They described this man warmly, but neglected to mention that he was old.

Isabella knew she could not resist, and so she agreed. On meeting her husband she was shocked at his age, but she was so charmed by his good manners and delicacy of concern for her that she decided she could bear to live with him if she must, but could never love him as she had her Lorenzo.

Soon after the wedding her maid servant came to her with news of a rumour that Lorenzo had not died of an illness but had been killed by the brothers while away on business for them, and that the grave was hidden in a corner of a wood nearby. So with her help Isabella went to the grave and found it covered in soft earth and leaves but without benefit of a headstone. She dug down and soon found the body of her poor lover. And in a moment of inspiration she took a knife she carried with her and cut off the part of him that had been most precious to her and wrapped it in a cloth, and the two stole back to their home that was now tainted with the stain of murder.

Isabella knew she could not be seen to act directly against her brothers, so she arranged to purchase a deadly poison that if given to them in small portions would slowly bring about their deaths. She compelled the servant to deliver this poison drop by drop in their food, telling her that if she did not do so she would betray her to her brothers, and she would suffer the same fate as had Lorenzo.

The servant did as she was told, slipping a drop or two of the poison into the meals of the brothers each day, who suspected nothing. And indeed they seemed pleased that their sister had overcome her grief and was settling into what looked to be a marriage that would bring them an ample return.

Isabella, to her own surprise, found much to enjoy in the company of her husband, not least in the details of his business affairs which he readily shared with her, believing her to be a worthy partner in the office as well as the bedchamber.

Within weeks the poison was having its effect as first one brother then the next fell ill, and shortly they died within a few days of each other. As a plague was causing much concern in the city no-one questioned their deaths, nor that of a servant woman at about the same time. Nor were they surprised when Isabella's husband died shortly afterwards of natural causes.

People were surprised, however, by the speed with which she took over the management of the men's many business concerns, and the skill with which she expanded them. She never married again, and shortly before she died she sold her businesses to a rival family, which flourishes to this day. Her great fortune was left to a distant cousin, whom she had hardly seen.

And so things come to pass.

But there is one more thing I have heard. During the preparations for her funeral a maid was going through Isabella's bedroom and came across a jewelled box at the back of a wardrobe. Inside was the shrivelled member of an unknown man, which she quickly threw away.

A Dream in Paradise

A long time ago, in a city not far from here, there lived a nobleman. He was a widower and had one daughter, named Andreola, whom he loved. Now, Andreola was beautiful and many men proposed to her, but no matter how her father tried to persuade her that this or that man would make a good match for her, she insisted she would only marry for love. 'Tosh,' said her father, 'You've been reading too many romances.' But while she might have been a romantic, she had a will of iron and remained adamant, much to her father's consternation.

Now, her father had a fine house with a beautiful garden that stretched all the way down to a river whose sparkling waters ran clear and bright. Andreola loved to walk beside it and listen while the birds sang and soft breezes gently stirred the blossoms of the pomegranate trees. And she did indeed love to read romances, often out loud to herself or to her maid who, though she could not read herself, took as much pleasure in the words and the sentiments as did her mistress.

One day Andreola noticed a young man working in the field beyond the river. Though it was clear he was not of her class, yet she was struck by his handsome bearing, which seemed nobler than his situation might suggest.

He had long fair hair and broad shoulders, and though his clothes were a little torn yet she could see he had a fine body, and she fell in love with him instantly. She asked her maid, 'Who is that man working there?'

'Why,' replied the maid, 'He is Gabriotto, the brother of my late cousin.'

'Hmm,' replied Andreola, 'Why is he working in the fields like a peasant?'

'Alas,' the maid replied, 'when my cousin died he left many debts and no children. Gabriotto was his only family, and now he must work the land himself, for he cannot afford to pay anyone to help him.'

'He looks too good for that,' said Andreola. 'Surely one so fine could not be born so low.'

'There were rumours,' replied the maid, 'that his mother had an affair with a noble count, and that he is in fact Gabriotto's father. But nothing could be proved.'

'Most unfortunate,' said Andreola. 'Might he come a little closer, do you think?'

'I'm sure his labours will bring him nearer, my lady. To within calling distance if I'm not mistaken.'

And indeed as the afternoon wore on the young man's labours brought him closer to them. And though no word passed between them, yet she was sure that he had noticed her and was drawn to her, for he seemed to spend an inordinate amount of time upon a patch of ground that was closest to her, weeding it carefully over and over again.

Her suspicions were confirmed when the next day, and the next, and indeed the one after, he lingered by the river bank, thus giving her ample opportunity to look upon him, and for him to send her in return soft and tender glances. Thus they declared their love.

Andreola's maid had been with her mistress some seventeen years, almost from the time of her birth, and she knew her mistress's thoughts before they were spoken. So she sent a message to Gabriotto that her mistress wished to speak with him about some matter and that he should cross the river by the little ferry and appear at the far end of the garden the next evening. Then, with very little difficulty, she persuaded her mistress to be walking there, so that they should meet. At first Gabriotto was shy before so grand a lady, and hardly dared to speak. But from their glances and the earnest entreaties that Andreola made to him to offer his services in her garden, insisting that no-one else would do, they contrived to meet again. To settle the matter, she also urged her father to hire the young man to bring about some lengthy transformation out of sight of the house where she knew he rarely came, so that she could look upon him and talk with him as often as she wished. And this being the spring, when the days are warm and summer's heat had not yet blistered the land, she arranged to read to him as he took his rest. He willingly surrendered, and she found in him a soul like her own, and their love-making began in earnest. And it was all her maid could do sometimes to mask their joyous cries as they consummated their marriage over and again.

But because theirs was a love match and entirely unapproved by her father, who remained ignorant of his daughter's bliss, it had to remain a secret; which gave them at first a delicious thrill, for as everyone knows, stolen kisses are sweetest. But soon a niggling desire crept into Andreola's mind, and she longed to be able to introduce her lovely young man to her friends and to see their envious stares as she walked with him to church or entertained them at her father's sumptuous table. Gabriotto for his part wanted to show her off to his friends at the local inn and to see his lands joined with hers so that he might act and be a gentleman to his beautiful lady.

So much did this desire trouble Andreola that she tried to think of ways in which her lover might be introduced to her father so that he might see him as she saw him. Yet she could not, and the turmoil inside her burned deep into her dreams, so that the normally pleasant recreations and embellishments therein – his sweet words, gentle caresses and bold moves towards her – turned dark within them. And thus one night in her sleep she saw arising from her lover as they lay together a black miasma, shapeless and stinking of the grave. The dreadful thing seemed to drag him away from her and draw him screaming down into the cold and lonely earth.

So disturbing was the dream that as the dawn broke she told her maid to send word to Gabriotto that she could not meet him that evening and that he must not look for her. Yet her heart broke as she did this, for she could not bear to be apart from him. And so, that night, as her yearning grew unbearable, she sent another message that she would meet him the next evening. And she remained awake till dawn for fear that the terrible mist would come and steal him from her again.

When they met their love-making was the more passionate for having been delayed by a single day. Then Gabriotto said to Andreola, 'My darling, why did you forbid me to see you last night? I was so concerned that you might have broken off our marriage that I was ready to kill myself!'

'Oh, heaven forbid that we should ever be parted,' she said, 'for ours is a love that belongs not only to this world but to the next as well.'

And so she told him about her dream, leaving out no detail, not even how he had struggled in vain against the fearful thing that took him kicking and screaming down into the earth.

Gabriotto could not help but smile when he heard this. 'That's strange,' he said, 'for I had a similar dream the very same night. I dreamed I had captured a beautiful young hind without need of arrows or spears but from my voice alone. And as I sat caressing the flanks of this beautiful animal one of my dogs, a fine black beast, the leader of the pack, suddenly turned on me and began to attack me. And though I tried to defend myself it managed to tear great pieces of my flesh from my body before it dragged me off. But as you can see, I am here in one piece. I've had many such dreams,' he said, 'and they all come to nothing.'

At this Andreola felt a cold wind briskly stir the trees, but she forced herself to smile about her foolishness in trying to see too much in them. And she embraced him again, and soon she forgot her fear in their love-making.

Only, it was to be their last, for as they lay together in each other's arms beneath the willow trees beside the river Gabriotto suddenly cried out in his ecstasy, 'God have mercy,' clutched his breast and without another word died.

Well, to say Andreola was distraught is hardly to guess the measure of it. Her lover, so fine, so full of life, so carefree, was suddenly dead - and not only dead but dead in her arms, and in her father's garden! It was if a dreadful premonition had come true and had wreaked a terrible vengeance upon them for the crime of being in love.

The sound of her mistress's cries attracted the attention of her maid, who as always was waiting nearby, ready to warn them if anyone should come near. She rushed to Andreola's side, and together they tried to rouse her lover. But it was no good. His beautiful body was already cooling as it lay stiff upon the ground.

Andreola was all for killing herself at this point just to be with him, but her maid spoke to her urgently: 'If you do you will never be able to join him, for suicide is the greatest sin, and he has surely gone to heaven. We must bury him and wait upon God's own time.'

For all her sorrow, Andreola knew her maid spoke the truth. But then how to bury Gabriotto's body without causing suspicion? Andreola wanted to do it there and then in the garden where so often they had celebrated their love.

'No,' said her maid. 'We will be discovered. Far better to take his body and leave it at his home. Then people will think he has died of some illness, and he will be buried innocent and free from sin.'

Her maid's words struck a chill in Andreola's heart for it touched upon the crime of their marriage, which had grown in the sunlight like a beautiful weed and had now died having shed its terrible seeds. But as she could see no alternative to the plan, she reluctantly agreed.

'I know where I can find a shroud,' her maid said. 'I'll fetch it and we can carry him over the stream in the little ferryboat he used to come to you. Then we can rest him on his cart and carry him home under cover of darkness while everyone else is asleep.' So she ran to the house while Andreola said fervent prayers over her lover's body. And surely no man was so deeply mourned as he, who had been taken from her even at the moment of their bliss. Such is the price of love.

When she returned they wrapped him up tenderly and dragged him to the waterside where they lifted him as best they could into the little boat. On the far side the maid said, 'It's best I sit here with the body till it is midnight. You go home and come back to me when the house is quiet. We dare not move now as we will be seen. Now go!'

Andreola was not used to being spoken to in this way by a servant, but she was in no fit state to argue, and so she did as she was told and ran swiftly to her room. There she wept and prayed for her beloved Gabriotto. And soon she fell into a deep and troubled sleep in which strange shapes without form or substance seemed to emerge from out of the ground and to mock her with their weird and frantic dances. And each time she tried to run from them they erupted again in front of her, like a forest fire that smoulders underground and bursts spontaneously into flame. This happened six or seven times, and would have carried on all night had she not woken with a start when the church clock struck twelve. Then, taking great care not to disturb the household she crept downstairs and out into the garden and down to the river bank. The moon was full and deep shadows lay in wait for her at the place where she and her lover used to meet, only now instead of seeming to embrace them they looked like great black mouths waiting to swallow her up. But she kept her nerve and pulled on the rope to draw the little ferry towards her.

When she got to the other side she called out for her maid: 'Where are you?' she said.

'Here,' the woman replied from somewhere in the bushes, and rustled the leaves to show where she was.

'Where?' cried Andreola, for at that moment a great wind had got up.

'Here mistress!' her maid replied. 'Before you!'

But Andreola could neither see nor hear her. As the wind blew harder and the trees took on strange shapes that mocked her senses and recalled the ghosts of her dreams, she tried to run towards the place from where she thought the voice had come, but she stumbled and fell. 'Where are you?' she cried, trying to rise out of the mud. 'Oh, where are you?'

'Over here!' she heard, faintly.

'Where?' she cried.

'Here, mistress!' The voice was suddenly beside her, and she looked up to see the face of her maid, as wet and bedraggled as she, staring down at her. 'I thought I had lost you.' the woman cried. 'How did this storm get up so quickly?'

'It's a judgement upon us,' Andreola cried.

'Maybe so,' said the maid. 'But there's still no time to waste. What will be, will be: we must finish what we have started.'

And so with grim determination and by clinging onto each other they set out against the storm, one pushing and the other pulling the little cart on which Gabriotto's body lay. And it seemed to them that it got heavier and heavier as they struggled through the mud.

Somehow they reached the place where the poor boy's house stood. It was not a grand house like Andreola's, but rather a shabby little cottage with a makeshift roof and a broken fence around it. When she saw it Andreola's heart was torn again, this time with pity. He had deserved so much: he could have been a prince in her world, but instead he had suffered because of her and had come to a dreadful end. And her tears mixed with the rain drops that poured down her cheeks.

Just as they were about to enter the house they heard a noise behind them and saw emerge from the shadows three men in black cloaks that flapped and shivered in the storm. The two women stood terrified and crossed themselves frantically, believing this was their end. 'Father, forgive me!' cried Andreola.

But instead of the voice of a demon they heard the sinister voice of the magistrate, whom Andreola recognised from a time when he had tried to propose to her. His words were not of love now. 'Arrest them!' he cried. 'Arrest them for the crime of murder!'

'What are you doing?' cried Andreola. 'We are not criminals. We haven't done anything!'

The magistrate merely sneered at them and ordered his men to open the shroud. On seeing the body of Gabriotto he ordered that they be taken to the town's jail, where they were placed in a cell. Andreola hid all night in the shadows in the furthest corner while her maid tried to comfort her. They had no food to eat or water to drink, and the place was as cold as the grave.

In the morning Andreola was summoned to the magistrate's office. She stood before him in her bedraggled clothes and was told to tell her story. Believing that a lie would only make her situation worse she told him the truth, hoping that as he was an official who had once taken an interest in her he would at least act honourably, even if he must execute the law.

But it was not to be. As soon as she had told him her story the magistrate insisted that she and her maid had murdered the young man and were planning to make it look like a natural death. And because this was almost the truth, and because Andreola was still consumed by guilt at the thought of her lover's death, she collapsed weeping upon the ground.

Things might have gone very badly for her had not the town's doctor then reported to the magistrate that no trace of poison or a wound could be found, and that Gabriotto had indeed died of natural causes. At this the magistrate changed his tune. 'As you are not guilty of murder,' he wheedled, 'I have it in my power to set you free. But I will do so on one condition.'

And with that he made a lunge at

Andreola and pushed her to the floor, where he would have ravished her had they not heard the voice of her father as he entered the building in search of his daughter.

'Where is she?' the Count demanded.

'In here,' cried the magistrate after a few seconds in which he managed to rearrange himself just enough to disguise his mischievous intentions. 'Your daughter is in here, under arrest.'

Her father strode in with a face like thunder and demanded to know by what right the little magistrate had been so impertinent as to arrest his only daughter.

Andreola ran towards her father, but the magistrate held her back.

'I arrested her on suspicion of

murder,' he said. 'And though I am satisfied she is not guilty of this crime, nevertheless she was in possession of the body of a handsome young man who is named Gabriotto. Moreover she has confessed to having an affair with him. A crime has therefore been committed.' And then the little scoundrel changed his tune. 'If you will allow me, sir, to spare you the threat of scandal I will marry your daughter forthwith and we need say no more about it.'

Unfortunately for him, the magistrate had underestimated Andreola's father, who dismissed his cunning little plan. 'Nevertheless, I demand to know the truth of what happened,' he said.

Andreola told him everything. She told him of her love for Gabriotto, how she had been afraid to speak of it for fear of his rejection, and her genuine sorrow at his death and the shame she had brought upon the family. And she told him of the magistrate's evil deed.

'My child,' said her father, 'I wish you had not kept this a secret. Perhaps you have learned a lesson. Let him be buried as fits his station. But to preserve your good name and mine you must renounce the world and find in the love of God the love you bore this unhappy man.'

The magistrate made one more appeal to marry Andreola, but he was silenced with a simple threat to expose his wicked deed.

Andreola had no choice but to accept her father's judgement. She and her maid both entered a convent where she soon became Abbess and did many good works. Her father died childless, and the magistrate rose to be a professor of law and married a woman whose ambition outstripped his own and kept him hard at work till he died of a stroke late one night alone in his office.

A Song for the Ferryman

… Come along now, come along, ladies and gents. Let's see your money. Yes sir, that's right, this is the boat to Hell. I'm Charon, your ferryman. No, Charon, with a Ch. Not a Sh. Do I look like a Sharon? Thank you. No, madam, there is no first class. We're all the same down here, as you'll soon find out. Yes, love, I've had 'em all. Politicians – plenty of them. Royalty. Businessmen. Rock stars.

…Who's the best passenger I've ever had? Well, there's so many. But there is one that stands out. Shall I tell you about him? The tide's not quite up so we've got a minute.

So, who do you reckon it was?

Someone really special. No, not Hitler, he came down ages ago. Works in the library now. No, go on. Guess. No? Only bleedin' Orpheus. Straight up! Biggest bloody rock god on the planet.

…What's that? You didn't know he was dead? Well, he isn't. That's my point. So, what was he doing down here? Good question. Let me tell you.

You see, this was a few years ago, before he made it big. He was just playing little clubs then, pubs, that sort of thing. What they used to call paying your dues. Yeah, I know, it's not like that now. Nowadays bands are all made up by computer. But then, then it was real music. What you call Old School. Rock and Roll! We get quite a few rock stars down here, what with the lifestyle and all. So in one sense I wasn't surprised to see him. But I could see straight away that him and his mortal soul were, like, still getting it on. So, I says to him, 'Hello mate. You're early!'

Turns out he's looking for his missus, Eurydice, who I'd carried over just the day before. He wants to ask old Hades if he can have her back. 'Good luck,' I said: 'He's a miserable old bugger, even if he has got Persephone for a wife.'

You see, Orpheus and Eurydice had just got wed, only part way through the reception she'd gone out for a breath of fresh, and she accidentally stepped on a snake. And this snake, not taking kindly to being stepped on, had bit her on the ankle. And that was it. Poor girl.

No matter what he did, she was on the road to hell, so to speak. I did think of telling him that they all come to me in the end, but then I thought, no. 'Cos I could see he was proper shook up. Well, he had just lost his wife, and she was a lovely girl. So, I'm not surprised he was so upset.

What's that? You heard? It was in all the papers. Yeah, I know. But I bet you don't know the whole story. It was kept quiet at the time, but as you lot ain't going nowhere it won't hurt if I tell you.

So, there he is, standing before me, and I say: 'Sorry mate, I've got rules. I can't take just anyone over into Hell. Imagine if word got out, they'd be queuing up for miles, just wanting to get a look at what's ahead of them.'

Do you know what he says? He says, 'If I play you a tune, man, will you take me over?' I said, 'It better be a good one, with a proper riff to it. Not the bloody rubbish they do nowadays!'

And so he gets out his guitar and he starts to play. And I thought, if you can play like that boy no wonder she's fallen for you. It was beautiful. He was running up and down the strings like a bloke possessed. Brilliant. Good as Hendrix. Better! And I gets to hear him every day.

So, I says, 'All right then, you've talked me into it. But just this once, mind.' Though frankly I didn't reckon much to his chances. Like I said, old Hades is a miserable old git and he's heard every excuse that's going. So, I was a bit surprised when Orpheus turns up again the next day, still alive, and begging me to take him over again.

I said to him, 'You've got a nerve, lad. Turned you down, did he?'

But he said, 'No.' And he told me what happened. He said he'd gone before Hades and his missus and he'd offered to play them a tune if they'd let Eurydice go back up top with him. He said at first old Hades wasn't having it, but Persephone, being a bit of a rock chick herself, persuaded her old man to have a listen.

And it works. He said he must have played the best gig of his life. Which would have been something, 'cos like I said, he can really spank the plank. And he was just about to walk off stage, so to speak, when Hades whistles him back. 'Oy,' he says. 'You can have her, but if you look back just once on the way out she comes back to me. All right?'

'All right!' says Orpheus, thinking this'll be easy. And so they sets off hand in hand, happy as Larry. But – and this is the sad bit – on the way up she falls behind, 'cos she's still limping from that old snake bite. And he gets worried, 'cos he can't hear or see her. And just as he's about to step out into the light he looks back. And that's it. She's gone. Done for. Poor girl. All he can hear is her cries as she goes back down again, down into the underworld, down into the dark and the cold.

So there he was, telling me the story. He'd come back again, hoping I'd take him across again. But, I had to say no, didn't I? I mean, I'd broken the rules once, I didn't dare do it again. So I said, 'Sorry mate. You'll have to wait your turn like everyone else'. Which, if rock and roll's still got any balls in it, won't be long.

So that's how Orpheus came to lose his missus. Which might seem hard, but at least he got some decent tunes out of it. He formed Orpheus and the Underworld, and they released their biggest hit, Snake Bite, and the rest, as they say, is history. He even wrote one for me: Song for the Ferryman. I was touched, I don't mind telling you.

I thought of selling my story to the

papers once, but was reminded by him
inside that I'm bound by data
protection. But Orpheus will be down
again soon, I expect. So, it don't matter
me telling you. 'Cos, like I say, you ain't
going nowhere. So, come on, move on
down the boat now. Pass me that oar.

The Raven's Command
A play for two voices

The scene is a church confessional. The era is medieval.

THURSTAN   Forgive me Father, for I have sinned.
PRIEST   Indeed, you have, my son.
THURSTAN   You have heard?
PRIEST   You seek sanctuary in my church. You have done something bad. If I am to grant you sanctuary I must have a full account.
THURSTAN   A full account? That'll take a long time, Father.
PRIEST   Just stick to the most recent events, my son.

THURSTAN I wanted a woman, Father.
PRIEST Many have, my son. Is that all?
THURSTAN I proposed to her in vain.
PRIEST That is surely no great sin. Is there nothing more?
THURSTAN She was proud, Father. She rejected my offer.
PRIEST Did she? And what was that my son?
THURSTAN Why, Father, I offered her marriage.
PRIEST Really? And?
THURSTAN I'm a rich man, Father. I'm not usually denied.
PRIEST Have you been married before?

THURSTAN   Three times, Father.
PRIEST   Indeed. And what happened? To your wives, I mean.
THURSTAN   They passed away. Well, one was divorced.
PRIEST   They had fortunes, no doubt.
THURSTAN   Of course, Father.
PRIEST   Of course. And what of this particular woman? Is she the reason you seek sanctuary?
THURSTAN   Yes, Father.
PRIEST   She is a remarkable woman?
THURSTAN   To be sure, Father, she is beautiful. But she denied me.
PRIEST   Well, well! Tell me more.

THURSTAN   I presented her my credentials.
PRIEST   How romantic.
THURSTAN   My offer was a good one.
PRIEST   I'm sure.
THURSTAN   I'm a rich man.
PRIEST   So you said.
THURSTAN   I knew her to be much like myself in character.
PRIEST   Much like yourself? You mean she does not give compliments easily? She tends to see the worst in people before the good. A bit of a cynic, perhaps? Is that what you mean?
THUSTON   You know her?
PRIEST   There are some like her, my son.

THURSTAN   But she turned me down.
PRIEST   Now why would she do that?
THURSTAN   I don't know.
PRIEST   Are you sure that's the whole story?
THURSTAN   The gist of it.
PRIEST   Did you not, how shall I say, demand she accept your offer?
THURSTAN   Well?
PRIEST   And did she not deny you outright, saying you had more chance of getting into bed with the Queen than with her?
THURSTAN   Yes, but
PRIEST   And did she not barricade herself in her room when you

tried to force yourself upon her?

THURSTAN   I'm a passionate man, Father. It's only natural.

PRIEST   And then when you protested and stormed about the place in an unholy rage threatening to tear the place apart, did she not say she could not give her hand to anyone who would not give her their heart?

THURSTAN   Yes! I took that as a load of rubbish. I had no intention of giving my heart to her or anyone else.

PRIEST   I'm sure she was aware of that, my son. And what did you do then?

THURSTAN   I returned home.

PRIEST   But surely you don't lack courage, my son?

THURSTAN   No indeed! I

wanted to make a plan. I was not going to be denied.

    PRIEST   Of course not.
    THURSTAN   I swear!
    PRIEST   What red blooded man would not? And did you?
    THURSTAN   What?
    PRIEST   Make a plan?
    THURSTAN   Sort of.
    PRIEST   Sort of? Did something not come to you?
    THURSTAN   Yes, Father. A raven.
    PRIEST   A raven?
    THURSTAN   Yes. A big black one.
    PRIEST   I think you'll find that if you look carefully they're a rather handsome shade of blue.

THURSTAN   Blue?

PRIEST   Yes, blue. Very fetching in the right light. But no matter. Continue. You say a raven came to you?

THURSTAN   Yes. And it spoke to me, as clearly as you are speaking to me.

PRIEST   Indeed. Like this? *(Imitates Thurstan's own voice)* Thurstan! Thurstan!

THURSTAN   Yes. Just like that! How did you know?

PRIEST   Just a guess. Carry on.

THURSTAN   Well, I thought I was dreaming. But it was so clear, I can't be sure.

PRIEST   That's the idea.

Carry on.

THURSTAN   I dreamed that as I sat thinking by the fireside I saw it pecking at my window.

PRIEST   Yes?

THURSTAN   Yes. And so I let it in.

PRIEST   People often do.

THURSTAN   Do they?

PRIEST   People often interact with animals in their dreams.

THURSTAN   Really? Has this happened before?

PRIEST   Oh, very often. What did it say?

THURSTAN   It said, you know you can beat her at her own game.

PRIEST *(imitating THURSTAN's voice again)*   You should go

down to the churchyard and there you will find a man who has recently been buried.

THURSTAN   Yes, that's it, exactly!

PRIEST   What else did it say, my son?

THURSTAN   It said: Dig down and open the shroud and with your knife cut out this man's heart and present it to her instead.

PRIEST & THURSTAN *(together)*
     See how she likes that!

THURSTAN   Hang on a bit. How do you know so much?

PRIEST   It's my calling to know such things. So what did you do?

THURSTAN   I did as I was told.

PRIEST   Of course. I knew you would.

THURSTAN   You did?

PRIEST   People always do. And you gave her this heart, claiming it was your own?

THURSTAN   Yes, Father. Mine was still beating inside me.

PRIEST   For now.

THURSTAN   Pardon?

PRIEST   You never know. Death comes when it is least expected.

THURSTAN   Not me, Father! It'll have to get up early to catch old Thurstan !

PRIEST   I could do with a penny for every time I've heard that. Never mind. Carry on.

THURSTAN   It looks like you

know the story.

PRIEST I?

THURSTAN Yes, you. Perhaps you can tell it?

PRIEST What, how you presented her with the heart, thinking your little gesture would somehow teach her a lesson, maybe even impress her with your wit, your boldness? A forthright man like you? A strong man, a man of action? With a sense of humour.

THURSTAN Maybe.

PRIEST And how she said she could never marry someone who had done so terrible a thing. And how she had said what she had said just to make you go away. And just then…

THURSTAN What?

PRIEST   Go on. It's your story.

THURSTAN   Oh yes. There was a terrible hue and cry outside the house.

PRIEST   There was a great crowd.

THURSTAN   An angry crowd.

PRIEST   A very angry crowd. They had discovered that a grave had been robbed. That the heart of someone dear to them had been stolen by some villain, some low criminal who could not even respect the dead. And now they wanted revenge.

THURSTAN   How did they know?

PRIEST   That it was you?

THURSTAN   Perhaps someone saw me?

PRIEST   A bird, perhaps? A raven? You can never trust them. Ravens.

THURSTAN   Ravens don't talk, Father.

PRIEST   Yours did.

THURSTAN   So it did.

PRIEST   Carry on.

THURSTAN   I expect you know what happened then.

PRIEST   What, how you made haste to the church, where you took sanctuary? Here, in fact?

THURSTAN   Yes.

PRIEST   And do you know what happened then?

THURSTAN   You mean there's

more?

PRIEST Oh yes.

THURSTAN Tell me.

PRIEST An angry crowd is a wondrous thing, my son. It has a beauty all its own. A savage beauty.

THURSTAN It does?

PRIEST It does.

THURSTAN How do you mean?

PRIEST Well, a crowd does not think. There's nothing clever about a crowd. Or reasonable. It just acts. It's all instinct, answerable to no-one. Anything can happen.

THURSTAN Oh!

PRIEST There's no calling it in, my son. Once you let it loose you can't just whistle it back. Once a mob gets it into its head it wants blood it will have it, any which way it can.

THURSTAN   They were after my blood?

PRIEST   They weren't fussy. Anyone's would do. But you were quick, were you not? You made haste to the church, where the law of sanctuary applies.

THURSTAN   I'm not stupid.

PRIEST   And so the mob broke in to the woman's house, and they found the heart there on the floor, where you had dropped it.

THURSTAN   They did?

PRIEST   They did.

THURSTAN   What happened then?

PRIEST   Why, they turned on the woman. I told you a mob

doesn't see reason or stop to think. They dragged her out kicking and screaming, and hanged her on the spot. Oh, they had some fun while they were at it, too. You said you thought she was an attractive woman?

THURSTAN   I did.

PRIEST   So did they. Much as you did, in fact, only rather more forcefully. But then there were more of them. She couldn't turn them all down.

THURSTAN   So…that's it then? It's all over?

PRIEST   Indeed.

THURSTAN   Can I go?

PRIEST   Of course.

THURSTAN   Thank you, Father.

PRIEST   Only, take care if you leave the church.

THURSTAN   Why's that, Father?
PRIEST   A little bird told them that the man they should be looking for is hiding here. You can hear them coming now, I think.
THURSTAN   My God! They'll kill me.
PRIEST   Very likely. But you'll agree there is a kind of justice in the matter?
THURSTAN   How do you mean?
PRIEST   What goes around comes around, wouldn't you say? Maybe you'll have time to make a proper confession before they hang you. I believe that's the parish priest coming out of the vestry now. If you're quick you'll just catch him. Now, I must fly!

Printed in Poland
by Amazon Fulfillment
Poland Sp. z o.o., Wrocław